Randolph Witherspoon was bored.
He wanted to take a walk.

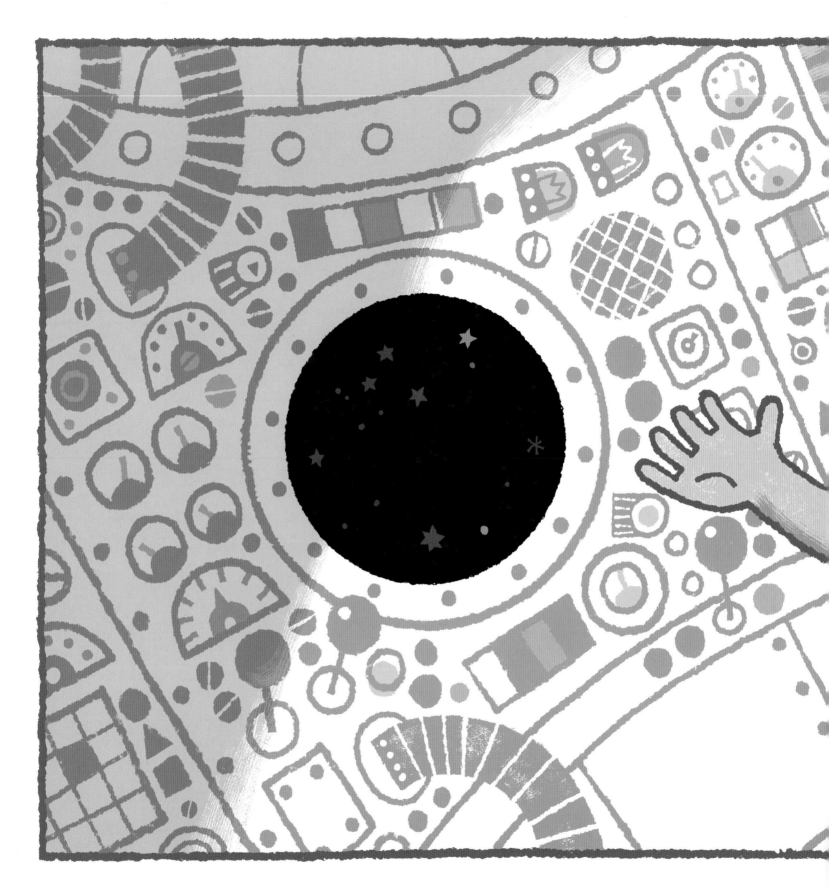

"I'm bored and I want to take a walk," Randolph complained to Ground Control, back on Earth. "Requesting permission to go outside."

He waited for a reply.

"Eat some lunch, get some exercise, and clean the place up a bit,"
ordered Ground Control. "Then you can go outside."

So Randolph ate some lunch.

He got some exercise.

He cleaned the place up a bit.

"Clear for spacewalk," said Ground Control. "Dress warmly, don't forget your camera, and be back before dinner!"

"Roger that," said Randolph as he suited up.

"And one more thing . . ." came the voice from Earth.

"Don't talk to strangers!"

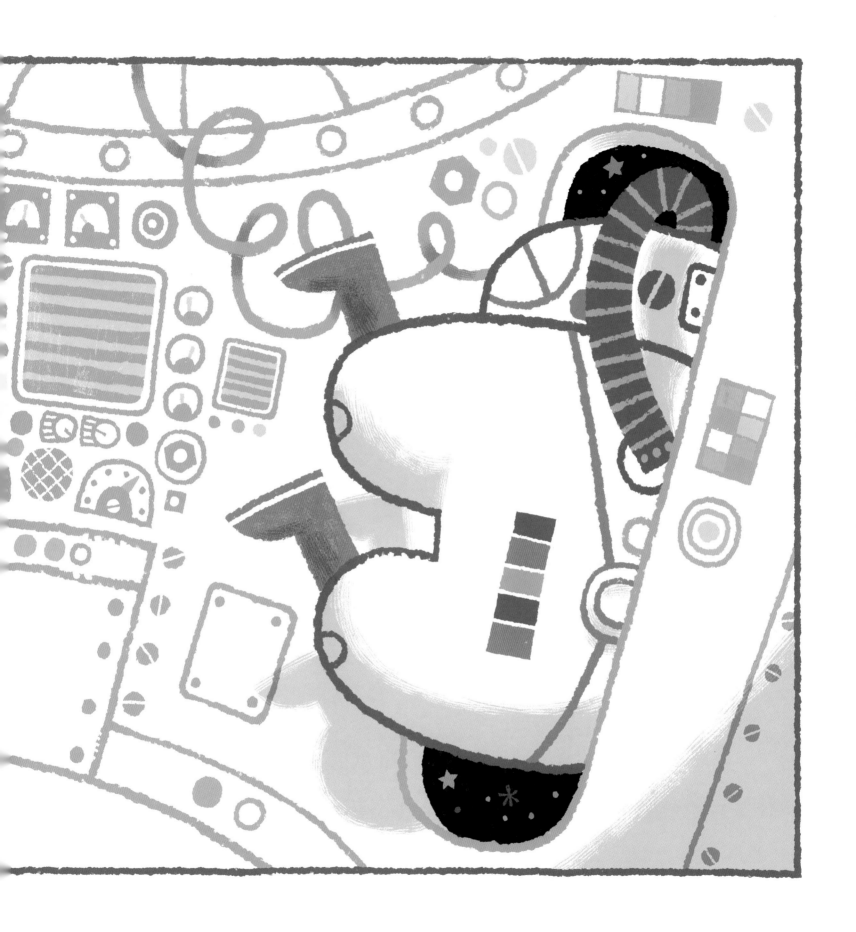

But Randolph was already out the door.

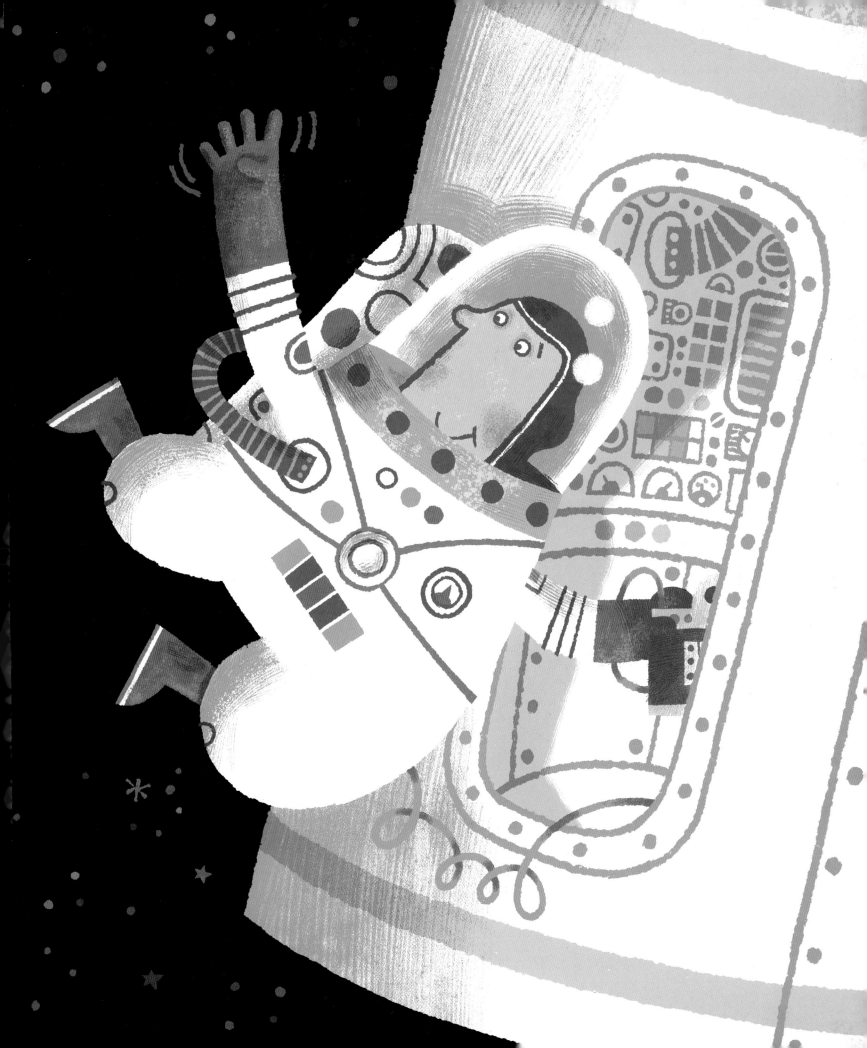

"Spacewalk complete!" said Randolph as he returned to the ship. "You're late," Ground Control replied. "Write your report, eat some dinner, and get some sleep."

"Then can I go out again?" asked Randolph.
"We'll see in the morning," replied Ground Control.

So Randolph wrote his report.

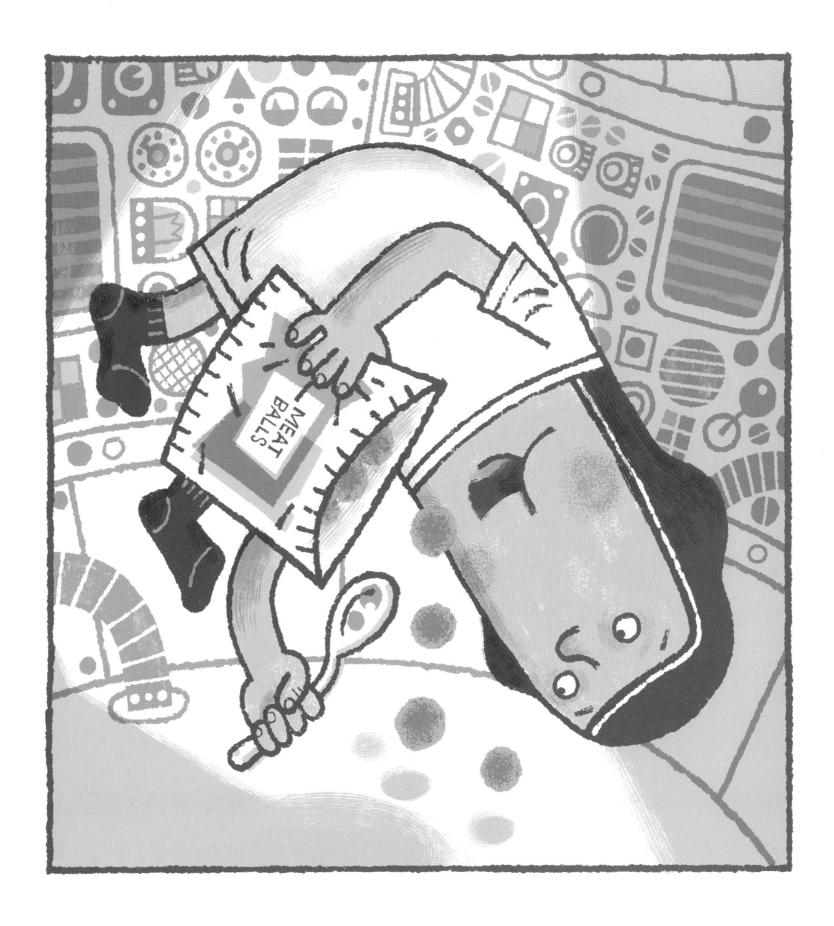

He ate his dinner.

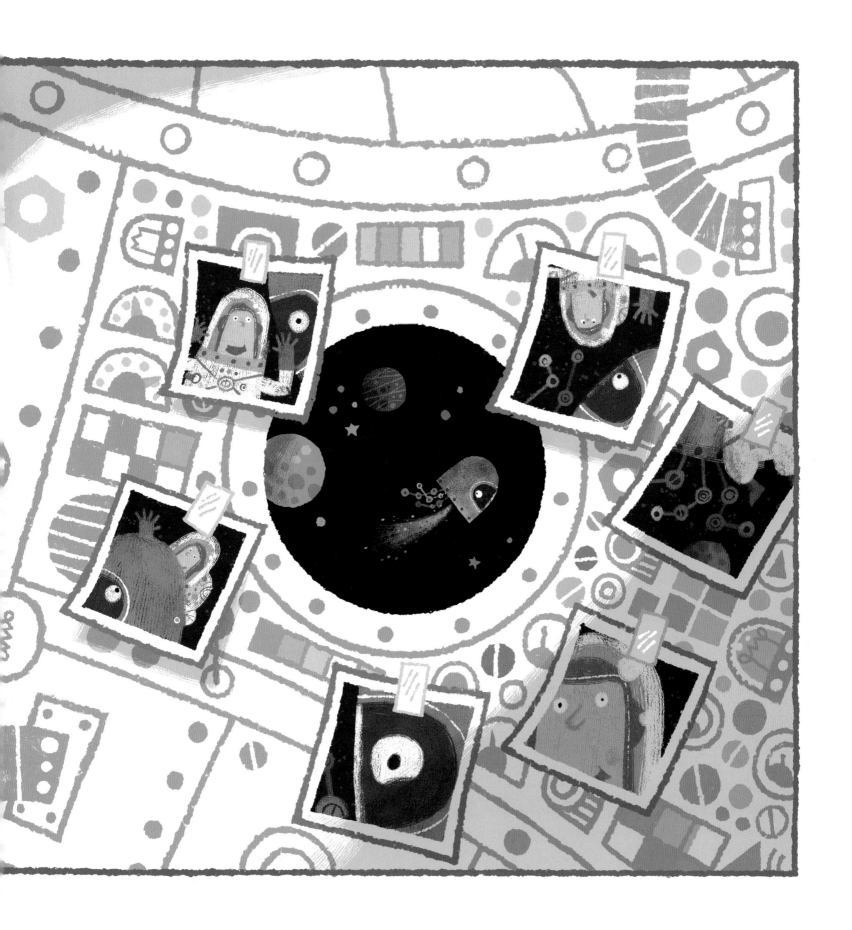

And he couldn't wait for tomorrow.